Not I, Not I

Modern Curriculum Press

BEGINNING
TO
READ
Series

Not I, Not I

Margaret Hillert

Illustrated by Diana Magnuson

ISBN: 0-8136-5563-3
Printed in the United States of America

18 19 20 21   06 05 04

Modern
Curriculum
Press

Pearson Learning Group

1-800-321-3106
www.pearsonlearning.com

Here is a mother.
The mother is little.
The mother is red.

Look here.
Here is a little baby.
The baby is yellow.
It can run and play.

See the yellow baby run.
See it run to Mother.
It said, "Mother, Mother.
I want something."

Mother said, "Come and look.
Help me find something.
Away we go."

Look, look.
Here is something.
Something little.
I can work.
I can make it big.

Oh, oh.
Look here.
One, two, three.
Can you help me?

11

Not I.
Not I.
Not I.
We can not help.

12

13

I can.
I can work.
See it go down here.

14

Look, look.
See where it is.
It is up.
It is big, big, big.

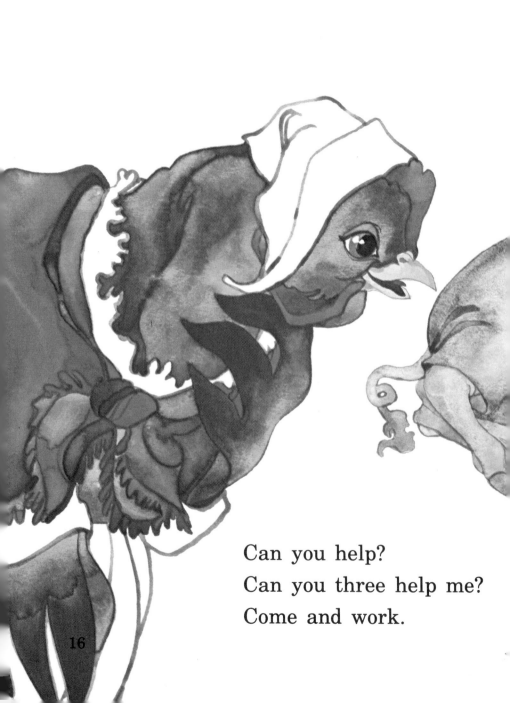

Can you help?
Can you three help me?
Come and work.

Not I.
Not I.
Not I.
We can not help.

19

It is funny.
You can not work.
You can not help.
I can work.

Here I go.
Away, away.
Can you come?
Can you help?

Not I.
Not I.
Not I.
We can not help.

See, see.
It is in here.
I can make something.

I can work.

See me work.

I can make something.

Look here, baby.
It can go in here.
It is for you.

Here it is.
Come and look.
Oh, oh.
Can you help me?

I can.
I can.
I can.
We can help.

28

Oh, oh.
We see it.
We want it.

Not you.
Not you.
Not you.
Go away.
It is for my little baby and me.

Margaret Hillert, author and poet, has written many books for young readers. She is a former first-grade teacher and lives in Birmingham, Michigan.

Not I, Not I uses the 44 words listed below.

a	help	oh	up
and	here	one	
away			want
	I	play	we
baby	in		where
big	is	red	work
	it	run	
can			yellow
come	little	said	you
	look	see	
down		something	
	make		
find	me	the	
for	mother	three	
funny	my	to	
		two	
go	not		